Look what's inside!

P56

Hi, girls,
It's me, Pepper!
I've got loads of fun
stuff for you in the
Animals and You
Annual! Take a peek
at some of the cool
things inside...

Have fun with these pet puzzles!

P6

These crazy cuties will make you LOL!

P42

P26

Great tips for learning how to ride!

P11

P54

Hi-Bear-Nating
Check out these Polar bear facts!

Aaw - This rescued rhino is so cute!

P34

Wanna know what your pet's saying? Find out here!

P46

Chi-Chi Bell's Story!
You'll ❤ her rescue pup story!

All this plus cute posters, fab photo stories and loads more!

Dolphins Make A Splash!

P-p-p-pick out a penguin!
There are six penguin pics hidden throughout the annual.
Can you spot them all?

Crazy Cuties!

These mad animals will make you giggle!

The kitty litter's that-a-way!

This could be a cat-astrophe!

Tickle me. Right now!

I want to phone a friend!

6

Your Year!

Had a good year? Why not fill in the boxes to save your memories – it's fun!

MY FAVE OUTFIT

It's so cool!

Draw it or stick a photo in the box!

It made me laugh!

Write down the funniest joke you know.

SILLIEST JOKE I HEARD

FAVE TV STAR

I'm a star!

Look for a picture in a mag you can cut out and stick here!

© TongRo, Daj, Pixtal

Who's Your Best Baby Animal?

Find the perfect baby animal for you!

START | Do you like country walks?

— no → Do you love sports?
— yes → Are nature progs best?

Do you love sports?
— no → Do you like long lies?
— yes → Are you always on the go?

Are nature progs best?
— no → Are you scared of wild animals?
— yes → Have you lots of cuddly toys?

Do you like long lies? — no → **Are you always on the go?**

Are you scared of wild animals? — no → **Have you lots of cuddly toys?**

Do you like long lies? — yes → Do you hate being cold?

Are you always on the go? — no → Do you hate being cold?
Are you always on the go? — yes → Do you go out in all weathers?

Are you scared of wild animals? — no → Do you go out in all weathers?
Are you scared of wild animals? — yes → Are you a veggie?

Have you lots of cuddly toys? — yes → Are you a veggie?

Do you hate being cold? — yes →
Do you go out in all weathers? — no / no →
Are you a veggie? — yes →

Cute Kitten
A little kitty is your purr-fect partner! You'd both love cosying up on cold, wintry days.

Playful Puppy
It's fun and games all the way with you and a playful, cheeky pup would love to join you.

Bonnie Bunny
A cuddly bunny's your ideal pet. You'd take great care to keep him happy and healthy.

Cute red blanket and sun block on his ears

Feeding time!

Carried to safety

RESCUED!
Maalim's story

Maalim, the baby rhino, was only a day or two old when he was found all alone in Kenya. There was no sign of his mother and he was very weak.

Luckily for Maalim, help was at hand. The little rhino was taken to the safety of the David Sheldrick Wildlife Trust. When he arrived, he weighed only 25 kilos and was just 205 mm tall. With expert keepers looking after him, he soon began to get stronger. He may still be tiny but he's a big favourite with everyone!

Maalim with a young friend

For more information on Maalim visit
www.sheldrickwildlifetrust.org

A Pet for

11 And one is before I go to school!

12 Next morning —

It's only six o'clock and I've got to get up!

15 But later —

Yeuk! Cleaning the cage is no fun though!

16 Then came Fluffy the cat —

At least you don't need walkies.

19 And so the following week —

Jazz was needing a home and I wanted a kitten, so we're both happy!

20 At last I have a pet of my own!

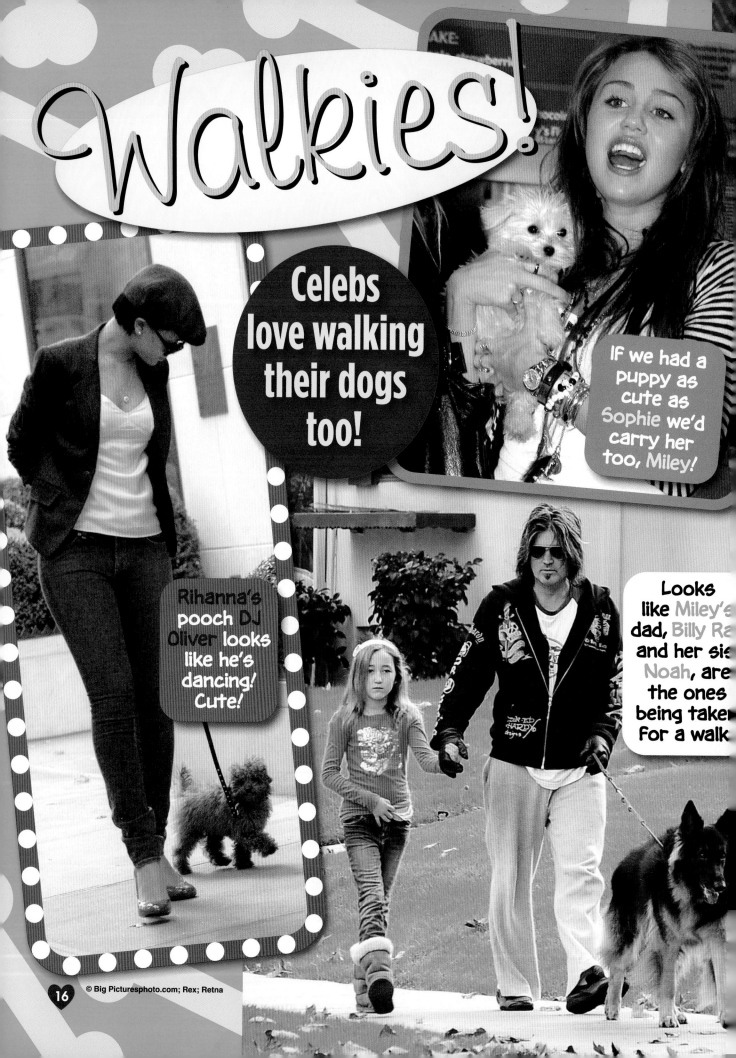

Walkies!

Celebs love walking their dogs too!

If we had a puppy as cute as Sophie we'd carry her too, Miley!

Rihanna's pooch DJ Oliver looks like he's dancing! Cute!

Looks like Miley's dad, Billy Ra and her sis Noah, are the ones being taken for a walk

There's a bit of a size difference between Nick and Kevin Jonas' dogs!

Bet Jessica Pussycat Doll won't walk too far in those heels!

Sarah from Girls Aloud's pooch gets used to the pup-arazzi!

I need shades too!

Paws rule!

Where's Hammy?

I'm hidden somewhere on these pages - can you find me?

18

What Kind of Bezzie Are You?

Take this fun quiz then give it to your mate to take too!

1 Your mate's forgotten to do her homework. Do you...?

a) Help her come up with a good excuse for not doing it. ☐

b) Give her a crash course on the homework topic so that she can hand in something. ☐

c) Let her copy yours - you don't want her to get in trouble. ☐

2 It's your BF's birthday, what prezzie do you get her?

a) That top she's been eyeing for weeks now. ☐

b) The perfect gag gift to make her giggle! ☐

c) You make her a photo album of all your fave memories - she'll love it! ☐

3 Which animal are you drawn to?

a) ☐ b) ☐ c) ☐

4 You pop round to visit your sick mate, do you...?

a) Bring your pet guinea pig for a visit - he always makes you feel better. ☐

b) Take round loads of games to cheer her up! ☐

c) Buy her the biggest box of the softest tissues! ☐

5 Your bezzie calls panicking over a test, you...?

a) Get her round for a movie marathon to take her mind off it! ☐

b) Reassure her - you know she'll do brill! ☐

c) Quiz her on her test so she'll be super-prepared. ☐

6 What are you and your bezzie gonna do this weekend?

a) Whatever your mate wants, you'll let her decide. ☐

b) You've got so many fun ideas it'll be hard picking just one! ☐

c) A trip to the zoo if the weather's nice. ☐

7 Your mate overhears the class bully saying something mean about her. Do you ...?

a) Give her a massive hug and tell her the bully is so wrong. ☐

b) Play pranks on the bully - she deserves it and it'll make your mate laugh! ☐

c) Confront the bully and tell her off for upsetting your mate. ☐

Now add up your score!

POINTS BOX

	a)	b)	c)
1.	2	1	3
2.	3	2	1
3.	1	3	2
4.	1	2	3
5.	2	1	3
6.	3	2	1
7.	1	2	3

IF you scored...

7-11 Caring Cat

Like a cute kitty you make a very caring mate! Your friends all love your sweet nature and the fact that you're always there to lend an ear, whenever they need to talk! Aaw!

12-16 Mad Monkey

You're a cheeky chimp who loves having a laugh. Your mates all think you're loads of fun to be around and you always cheer them up!

17-21 Protective Lion

You're like a lioness with her cubs - you always look out for your mates and stand up for them! You'd do anything to help a friend!

Get Puzzling!

HIDDEN BANANAS

There are six bananas hidden on these two pages. Can you spot them?

MIXED UP MONKEYS

These are all types of monkey but the letters have got jumbled up. Can you sort them out?

LOWLOY

PRIDES

ALFE

REQUILRS

LOW

SPOT THE DIFFERENCES

The pictures look the same but there are five small differences between them.

BABOON
BUSH BABY
CAPUCHIN
CHIMPANZEE
COLOBUS
GIBBON
GORILLA
HOWLER
LEMUR
LORIS
MACAQUE
MANDRILL
MARMOSET
ORANGUTAN
TAMARIN
TARSIER

WORDSQUARE

Find the listed animals hidden in the square – they're all primates. You can move forwards, backwards, up down or diagonally.

```
C O L O B U S N B T O R
A H X J K T N H A E F Q
P O I M Y B A B H S U B
U W D M E X T M I O Q A
C L M T P A U Q A M R B
H E S A Y A G K A R E O
I R I Y N O N C N A I O
N U R Q R D A Z R M S N
J M O I A Q R F E R R E
L E L U U V O I M E A M
Y L S E T X F M L C T C
A N O B B I G M Z L A M
```

CHIMP OR CHUMP?

How much do you know about chimps? Which is true and which is false?

CHIMPS ...only eat fruit? ...always walk upright like humans? ...usually sleep in trees? ...are endangered? ...are only found in parts of India?

ANIMAL RECORD BREAKERS

Check out these fantastic facts about some amazing animals.

I can't wait till they've grown up and left home!

Super mum!

Button the Dalmatian had a record 33 pups in two litters! Here she is with her second litter of 18 little cuties. Bow-wow!

Fastest ferret!

Warhol the ferret ran 10m in 12.59 seconds. Speedy or what?

Ready, steady.... let me go!

High There!

I get a great view from up here!

The tallest giraffe ever was 5.8m tall - almost as high as two double decker buses!

Egg-straordinary!

An ostrich laid the largest egg on record - 2.58kg. **Wow!**

Super mum 2!
A record 19 kittens were born to a Burmese/Siamese cat in 1970. What a handful!

Zzzzz!
The sleepiest mammal ever must be the pygmy possum who hibernated for 367 days. **What a sleepyhead!**

Porky jumper!
Kotetsu the pig jumped 70cm in Japan in 2004, the highest pig jump ever recorded. Very pig-culiar!

You could make lots of omelettes!

I'm starving now!

Big ears!
The longest dog's ears belonged to **Tigger** the Bloodhound. His ears were 34.9cm and 34.2cm long. The longest rabbit's ears measured 79cm! **Unbelievable!**

I'm training for the Olympics!

Will *my* ears grow that big?

Making A Splash!

Why dolphins are totally amazing!

In New Zealand, a bottlenose dolphin called Moko saved two stranded whales by guiding them off a sand bank and safely out to sea!

Dolphins can solve problems and use tools! Some Australian dolphins carry sea sponges to protect their beaks from spikey sea urchins!

They can point to objects with their heads to lead humans to them!

Researchers have found that swimming with dolphins can help people who are feeling sad or ill.

Dolphins are thought to be more intelligent than humans!

Dolphins in Australia tried to warn boys who were surfing about a tiger shark – then chased the shark away!

'Dolphin therapy' can help people with health problems or disabilities. Children who have trouble speaking have even been known to say words after playing with dolphins!

I Wanna be a Volunteer!

Shannon loves animals so we took her along to a Scottish SPCA animal centre to help out!

I can't wait to meet the other animals!

3 SSPCA Officer Lesley helped Shannon check over new arrival, Patch the guinea pig...

First, you have to check mites...

7 Time to start grooming the animals!

Olive loves being brushed...

HOT or COLD?

Look for these amazing creatures in the wordsearch.

When you've found them all, sort out who lives in the hottest and who lives in the coldest places in the world.

ALBATROSS
ARCTIC FOX
CAMEL
CARIBOU
COYOTE
GAZELLE
ORCA
GERBIL
HARP SEAL
KANGAROO
MONGOOSE
PENGUIN
POLAR BEAR
DINGO
WALRUS

```
U F K W P E N G U I N
C Q K L T G E R B I L
L Y X O F C I T C R A
Q E Y F G A Z E L L E
D O M S G O A A B L S
C I R A E B R A L O P
Q B N C C I T L L S R
K A N G A R O O L C A
N I B U O B I R A C H
C I T S U R L A W O S
H E S O O G N O M R L
```

Answer:

Hottest camel, coyote, gazelle, gerbil, kangaroo, mongoose, dingo,

Coldest albatross, Arctic fox, caribou, orca, harp seal, penguin, Polar bear, walrus.

Spot The Difference

©Daj.

Answers

5. Ball of wool is a different colour.
4. Lid of box is a different colour.
3. Extra pom pom.
2. Heart shape on the front of the box.
1. Left eye is a different colour.

31

Wonder if **Corbin** will be the **mane** star of his next movie?!

This spaniel has stolen **Leona Lewis'** hairstyle!

Totally

Some of our fave stars

She stole my hair!

Ashley's We reckon turning into **Boi**, her cutie-pie **HSM** co-star!

MY eye make-up's the coolest!

Avril's

We ❤ panda eyes... and so does the panda!

Twins!

Rihanna's

been **spotted** looking wild!

look just like animals!

Jonas Brothers

look p-p-p-retty similar to these p-p-p-penguins!

© Photodisc; Rex; Quarto; Digital Stock; Purestock; John Foxx

What's Your Pet Saying?

How to understand your pet!

Cats

Scary Cats

Cats arch their backs to make themselves **look bigger** and scarier when they feel threatened. Their fur usually **stands on end** as well.

I'm purrfectly happy!

Cute Kitty

A cat will purr and knead with its paws if it's happy. Cats who roll over on their backs and show you their belly are saying 'I trust you'! Aaw!

Rabbit

What's Up, Doc?

If a rabbit is standing straight up on its hind legs, it's being curious and trying to see more of its surroundings.

Happy bunny

Rabbits **grind** their **teeth** softly when they're happy, just like a cat purring. They also love to **jump and dance** when they're happy and excited!

Dogs

Top Dog

If a dog feels threatened its fur will stand on end making it look bigger than it really is. If the other dog or human won't back down it'll wrinkle its nose and bear its teeth.

Wanna play?

Play Time!

A playful dog will have its head held low, its front paws stretched out and its bottom in the air. Its tail will be held straight up and be wagging excitedly – this is the signal for "I want to play" and it's known as the 'play bow'!

Horse

Ear ear

Keep an eye on your pony's ears if you want to figure out its mood! Ears usually point in the direction of the horse's attention, so when you're riding it's best if at least one ear is pointing back at you to show it's listening!

Check out its ears!

Watch Out!

Did you know that horses flatten their tail between their legs like dogs when frightened? Tail lashing can be a sign that they're irritated or annoyed and it's often followed by a kick!

BFFs
X

animals and you

★ Animal Heroes

These animals have big hearts!

Read on to find out all about them -

Tiny roe deer **Cindy** was found abandoned and taken to a rescue centre in Somerset.

Rocky a giant Great Dane whose owner works at the centre, quickly bonded with the little orphan fawn and started to act just like Cindy's mum!

Hero Rocky!

Thanks to Rocky, Cindy is happy and healthy!

Hero Luka!

Luka the German Shepherd had never had puppies, but when six rescued kittens were brought to a rescue centre, Luka became their Mum. The kittens had been saved from the Australian bush fires and thanks to Luka caring for them they have a happy future.

Hero Tia!

Tia the terrier was being looked after by friends Sonia and Roy when she woke Sonia up in the middle of the night. Tia had sensed that Roy was ill and luckily Sonia phoned the emergency services in time to save Roy's life.

This is one lucky hedgehog! Thanks to **Whiskers** the cat finding him asleep in a bonfire, he's still alive. The little hedgie was named **Smokey** and a wildlife hospital looked after him till he could be set free in the wild. Well done, Whiskers, for saving Smokey's life!

Whiskers wants to ask everyone to carefully check bonfires before lighting them in case there are any hedgehogs like Smokey sleeping in them.

Hero Whiskers!

Ashley And Maui

Make your own cool Ashley & Maui story

It was a .... day in L.A! Ashley yawned and stretched. "Wake up, Maui! We've got loads to do today. I'm going to wear my fave ....!" Ashley got up and bathed Maui with her fave bubble bath which smelled of..................... Mmm!
They had a delicious breakfast of .... and ....
Yum!

"Let's go shopping, Maui," said Ashley. I want to buy a cool .... and you need a new ....
The shops were fun! Ashley spent $............ on treats for her and Maui. Maui looked cute in her new, bright .... Which was ....
When they got home, they both got changed. "I'd love a .... flavour milk-shake Maui," Ashley sighed. "C'mon, let's go!"
The milkshake was ....!
Back home, Ashley quickly put on the pretty .... she'd bought that morning. "We're meeting Vanessa and Shadow at

the ...., sweetie," she told Maui. I'd better call Van on her mobile cos we're gonna be late!" After catching up with all the HSM gossip (Did you know that .... had a mega-cringey moment on the HSM set when

Let's shop till we drop!

Hit Hollywood!

by filling in the missing words!

*TIP:
You can fill in the words as many times as you like, to change the story – or even add silly words to make it funny!

she ....
....
..... over ....
....

Hi Ashley!

.... and
....
........................?
Oops!), Ashley had to hurry home to change AGAIN! She and Maui were appearing on a top TV chat show along with famous stars like
....
and ....
Cool!
First, Ashley went to the hairdresser. "I need a change please!". Maui thought Ashley's new dark hair colour looked ....!

Everyone on the chat show LOVED Ashley and Maui! Phew – now Ashley was feeling
....
Yawn!
Her long and
....
day wasn't over yet though – now she had to jump in a
.... and head straight to the airport with Maui. They were going on a

well-earned holiday – hooray! – to Ashley's fave holiday hotspot,
....
Lucky girls!!
At last, Ashley could snooze on the plane – Zzzzzzz!

Saddle Up With Amber

Amber Ross **loves horses.** Her friends, Anna, Rachel and Suzanna **go riding at stables nearby. Amber's joining them for her first lesson. Let's see how she gets on!**

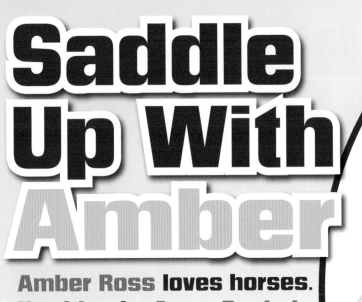

1

Amber meets Peach, the pony she's going to ride.

2

Anna shows her how to put Peach's headcollar on.

3

Grooming is important and Peach likes being brushed! Amber learns to use the hand nearest the pony's head.

Time to tack up. Anna helps Amber with the saddle.

4

5

Now to mount - with a bit of help from Kelly, the instructor.

6

Amber and Peach join Anna on Sienna and Rachel on Jet.

43

7 Suzanna leads Peach and Amber round the arena.

Hard hats should always be worn when handling or riding ponies.

8

Thanks, Peach! You're the best pony ever!

That was great! Peach deserves some pony nuts!

9

Amber had a fantastic first lesson. She's going back every weekend from now on!

Thanks to Hooves and Paws Riding School and Equestrian Centre, Stonehouse. www.hooves-and-paws.org

animals and you

Sienna x

Benji saved my life!

Benji

Rescued!

Chi-chi Bell's story

A very lucky Chihuahua called Chi-chi Bell is now fully recovered from her injuries and safe with her new owners, thanks to being rescued by Benji the German Shepherd cross.

Benji was out for his daily walk with Mick, one of the volunteers from Battersea Dogs and Cats Home, Old Windsor, when he pulled him over to a patch of hawthorn.

Mick thought that Benji had sniffed out a rabbit, but when he looked more closely, he found the tiny Chihuahua!

The little dog was taken to the Home where it was discovered she had a badly damaged leg and it's thought that she had been dumped nearby.

Chi-chi Bell, probably wouldn't have been able to find her way out of the thick bushes, and

without the help of Benji's keen nose and the care and attention from the staff at the Home, the story might not have had a happy ending!

Latest News!

Chi-chi Bell's doing really well and her new owners have given her a new name — Chilli Bean. How cute is that?

Santa Claws!

Can you guess the animals hiding behind the Santa Claus beards and hats?

a

b

c

d

Answers
a) bear, b) panda, c) tiger, d) cheetah

© purestock

47

In Your Dreams

Find out what your animal dreams mean...

Kitten

If you're mad about **kittens** and dream about them, it means you're creative and confident. You love being the centre of attention so much – maybe you're a star in the making!

Puppy

Looks like your life will never be boring, cos dreaming about a cute **puppy** means you're playful, fun to be with and will have loads of friends.

Duck

Dreaming about a **duck** means travel and you could be packing your suitcase soon. Look out for a fun school trip or an exciting family holiday! Cool!

Rabbit

Dreaming about **rabbits** is a sign of true friendship. It means you're a great mate and you also have lots of amazing bezzies that you can totally rely on.

Elephant

An **elephant** in your dreams means brain-power and a good memory. Definitely the animal you'd want to dream about if you've a tricky test coming up at school!

Squirrel

Lucky you if you see **squirrels** in your dreams! It means you'll have fun and happiness at home and you'll meet up with lots of new mates too!

Goat

Seeing a **goat** in your dreams means there's some extra cash coming your way. Cool - you can splash out on something new or a treat for your BFF!

HO! HO! HO!

Christmas jokes to make you LOL!

WE wish you a merry christmas...

What kind of bird can write? A pen-guin!

What kind of pet does Aladdin have? A flying car-pet!

What do monkeys sing at Christmas? Jungle Bells!

Who delivers presents to young sharks? Santa Jaws!

Why don't reindeer like penguins? Cos theycan't take the wrappers off!

What's a duck's fave Christmas food? Christmas quackers!

Who's never hungry at Christmas? A turkey, cos he's always stuffed!

What's a crocodile's fave Christmas party game? Snap!

What do sheep write in their Christmas cards? Merry Christmas to ewe!

Why is Rudlolf always wet? Cos he's a rain-deer!

animals and you

Santa Paws

© Daj

Relaxing inside or looking for adventures outside? Do this fun quiz and find out the animal you're most like!

Is playing practical jokes fun?

Yes

N

Do you love sleepovers?

Yes

No

Do you get up when you wake up?

Yes

Are you happiest reading a book?

Yes

Polar Bear

You're **energetic** and strong like a polar bear. You love sports and games and you'll have loads of fun outdoors no matter how bad the weather gets. Swimming in the pool or at the beach is a fave pastime.

No

Yes

start

Are you happy goin out in the rain?

Is ice cream better than cream cakes?

Yes

No

No

No

Do you look forward to games?

Yes

No

No

Can you keep secrets?

Koala

Koalas love to **sleep** and so do you, whether inside or out! Relaxing on a sun lounger is one of your favourite summer pastimes. And, in the winter, a bowl of **munchies** in front of the **TV** is your idea of fun.

Yes

Do you have long lies at the weekend?

Yes

Yes

N

No

Is summer best?

thrills?

What's your animal personality?

Yes → Are barbecues best?

Do you prefer cold drinks?

No ↓

Yes → Would you like a winter holiday?

No ↓

Are you first to wear shorts in Summer?

No →

No ↓

Yes → Is sun bathing better than swimming?

Is shopping fun?

Yes ↓   **Yes** ↑

No →   **Yes**

Do you love board games?

No →

No ↓

No ↓

Are you happy watching sports?

Yes ↑

Do you like cosying up with your pet?

Yes →

Yes ↓

Are you a tomboy?

No →

Penguin

You're a real **outdoor girl**! Sun or rain you're happy to be out in the fresh air. You're the first to wear flip flops as soon as the sun shines and just like the **penguin** you never seem to feel the cold!

Kitten

Like a **kitten** you just love curling up in bed or somewhere cosy with nothing to do. You don't like the rain or snow as they just mess up your hair! **Pampering** evenings with your mates is your favourite thing.

53

In autumn, female bears who are going to have cubs start to dig a den in the icy snow.

I'm off to build my den!

When the den is finished, Mum-to-be bear goes inside to hibernate.

Polar bears live on ice floes in the freezing cold Arctic Circle.

Hi-Bea

What's in Mu

Like all youngsters, the cubs have great fun playing in the snow and ice.

There are usually two cubs born. The twins are blind with no fur, so need to cosy into Mum to keep warm.

Baby bears are teeny and weigh less than half a kilogram — adult bears can weigh over 600 kilos!

During the winter, Mum gives birth to her cubs, usually when she's fast asleep!

r–Nating!

olar bear's secret den?

Mum and her cubs stay in the den until it's spring. When it gets warmer she takes her cubs out of the den for the first time.

Brr! It was warmer in the den!

The cubs stay with their mum for over two years, until they are able to look after themselves.

55

Pet Puzzles!

Spot the Differences?

Can you spot the six differences in these two pics?

Moggy Maze

Poor Princess has been searching everywhere for her fave sparkly collar. Can you help her through the maze to find it?

Start

Hidden

There are six hammies hidden about the page. Can you find them all?

Answers on page 68

Pet Search

Can you find these pet animals in the word search? Words can read up, down, backwards, forwards and diagonally. The word **pet** appears more than once. How many can you find?

Rabbit
Kitten
Mouse
Guinea Pig
Hamster
Budgerigar
Goldfish
Pony
Puppy
Gerbil

I know the answer…

S	G	I	P	A	E	N	I	U	G
Y	M	L	T	E	P	U	P	P	Y
N	H	A	M	S	T	E	R	G	P
O	K	I	T	T	E	N	F	Q	E
P	H	S	I	F	D	L	O	G	T
T	E	P	E	T	S	S	T	E	P
J	L	I	B	R	E	G	P	E	T
R	A	G	I	R	E	G	D	U	B
T	I	B	B	A	R	F	P	E	T
P	E	T	E	S	U	O	M	H	P

All in a Scramble!

Can you unscramble these doggy breeds?

licelo

skuyh

eagbel

olmpitoa

I'm all muddled up!

Then place them in the grid and the shaded area will spell out Ashley Tisdale's famous pet pooch!

Pepper

3 Can you remember where you last saw it?

I think I had it just before I took Pepper out for a walk.

4 Hey, don't blame me!

7 Bye, Mum! Thanks again!

Just try not to lose anything else today, Lolly!

8 But after school —

Are you still looking for that homework?

Er, no. I'm looking for the mp3 player I got for my birthday.

59

Cool Creature

Mandrill

Mandrills are monkeys that are closely related to baboons and they have brightly coloured blue or red faces. Their skin colour gets even brighter the more excited they get!

Looks like he's been at the face paints again!

Blue Morpho Butterfly

Morphos have amazing metallic blue wings that flash in the sunshine as they fly through the rainforests where they live.

Not fair - the males are a much brighter blue than the females!

Blue Is Beautiful!

Blue shark

This shark has a bright blue body and a white underside and is the most common in the world! Blue sharks have a reputation as man-eaters and can attack and overpower whales and animals larger than themselves! Eek!

Don't mess with me!

Blue Peacock

The Blue Peacock is a brightly coloured pheasant from India with shimmering blue and green feathers. Whenever a peacock wants to attract a mate it turns its feathers into a gorgeous colourful fan around its body!

Let's party!

Did you know that a group of peacocks and peahens is called a party?

Colours
amazingly colourful!

Goldfish

Goldfish have a substance in their skin called 'guanine' that reflects light and makes them glimmer - just like gold! These pet fish actually come in many colours and sizes, not just the teeny orange ones we're used to!

Goldfish don't have eyelids so they can't close their eyes when they snooze!

© Purestock, Pixtal, Photodisc, Digital Stock.

Don't call me a carrot-top!

Did you know ... Tigers love to swim!

Orangutan

You might think that Orangutans were named after their long orange hair but their name actually means 'Person of the Forest'. That's because Orangutans spend most of their time up in the trees - they even sleep in them!

Tiger

These gorgeous big cats have thick orange fur coats with white bellies and black stripes all over their bodies. They may look brightly coloured but their striped coats let them blend in as they stalk through long grass.

Totally Orange Critters!

Orange cats

I'm a cute redhead!

Orange cats can be either pure ginger cats or tabby cats. A cat's colour depends on whether it is male or female. It's much more common to have a ginger tom cat than a ginger female cat. Some tabby cats also have stripy orange/gold fur.

It's In The Stars!

Find the year you were born and see what it says about your personality!

See what your Chinese starsign says about you!

THE LEGEND!

Chinese legend says the god Buddha asked all the animals on earth to come and see him. 12 animals came and he honoured each animal with a year, which is why there are 12 animals in the Chinese calendar!

Born in 1996
Year of the RAT

RATS are so POPULAR cos they're FUN to hang out with! You're very GENEROUS and love to surprise your friends with treats! You'd make a good AUTHOR or ARTIST cos you have a great IMAGINATION!

Born in 1997
Year of the OX

If you're an OX, people love you cos you're SWEET and SHY! You're also very CLEVER and good with your HANDS so you'd make a fab SURGEON or HAIRDRESSER!

Born in 1998
Year of the TIGER

TIGER girrrrrls are BRAVE and love ADVENTURES! You're so sporty and aren't scared to take RISKS or STAND UP for yourself. You'd be a brilliant BOSS or EXPLORER!

Born in
1999
Year of the RABBIT

RABBITS are KIND and CUDDLY. You're such a SOFTIE, no wonder you have loads of FRIENDS! Someone as CHATTY and BUBBLY as you would make an awesome CHAT SHOW HOSTESS or ACTRESS!

Born in
2000
Year of the DRAGON

Wow! DRAGONS have so much ENERGY and just love to PARTY! You're mega POPULAR because you're so FUNNY – you'd make a great LAWYER or the best POLITICIAN ever cos everyone would vote for you!

Born in
2001
Year of the SNAKE

How did you get to be so SMART? You're very WISE and always give great ADVICE to your friends if they're upset. You'd make a perfect DOCTOR or TEACHER cos you're so PATIENT.

Born in
2002
Year of the HORSE

HORSES always WORK HARD and do their BEST! You're really INTELLIGENT and CREATIVE and with all your brains and cool ideas you'd make a top SCIENTIST or POET.

Born in
2003
Year of the SHEEP

SHEEP love NATURE and ANIMALS and prefer being outdoors. You're also fabulously FASHIONABLE and have great STYLE! ZOO-KEEPER or FASHION DESIGNER would be cool career choices!

COPY CATS

Be artist-fantastic! Copy the cute kitties into the grid below!

FACT OR FIB?

Can you guess which of the following are facts and which are fibs? You might be surprised!

1. **Ostriches** bury their heads in the sand when in danger

2. **Emus** can walk backwards as well as forwards

3. **Snails** can hibernate for three years

4. Touching a **toad** or **frog** can give you warts

5. **Bats** are totally blind

6. **Giraffes** clean their eyes and ears with their tongues

7. **Dolphins** sleep with one eye open

8. **Flamingoes** can only eat when their heads are upside down

9. **Honeybees** have hair on their eyes

10. **Snakes** see through their eyelids

Answers: 1.Fib, 2.Fib, 3.Fact, 4.Fact, 5.Fib, 6.Fact, 7.Fact, 8.Fact, 9.Fact, 10.Fact.

The animals and you AWARDS

TOP PET CHARITY

"I'm a rock princess!"
TOP TV SHOW

The PDSA helps out loads of sick pets – how good is that?

The Elephant Princess on *Nickelodeon* is the coolest!

Our faves from 2009!

CUTEST CELEB & PET
"How cute am I?"

Ashley and Maui win 1st prize!

FAVE FILM

We loved Bolt – and it was even better in 3D!

Miley Cyrus
MILES TO GO

BEST BOOK

We couldn't put down Miley Cyrus Miles to Go!

BEST WEB PAGE

We're addicted to www.clubpenguin.com!

POSHEST POOCH

Chloe from Beverly Hills Chihuahua!

Puzzle Answers (p56-57) Spot the Differences: Kitten on left missing ear and nose, Kitten on right missing paw, Sweet missing fom glass on left, Sweet missing from glass on right, Sweet missing on bottom right. Pet Search: 10 pets. All in a Scramble: Maltipoo, Beagle, Husky, Collie. Shaded Area: Maui

What's Your lucky animal?

Find out which cute creature brings you luck!

I can be a bit cheeky
START

I spend my pocket money too quickly

I get told off for day-dreaming

I often win prizes

I'm always last to be picked at school

Help! Homework's hard!

I want to find something I've lost

I'm always forgetting stuff

Purse £3, Claire's

monkey
You need help with managing money! Stash your cash in a cheeky monkey purse for loads of luck!

Kitten phone charm £1.50, Claire's

cat
You need big help to get your luck back! A cute kitten charm will help you win a prize and come first for a change!

Dolphin earrings £3.50, Claire's

dolphin
You're always in a dream and schoolwork can suffer! Dolphin earrings will bring good fortune and help you concentrate!

69